Princess Pru
and the Ogre
on the Hill

For my pals, Jodi and Colleen—M.F.
For my wife, Elena, whose home city of Alicante inspired the scenes in this book—D.M.

Text © 2023 Maureen Fergus
Illustrations © 2023 Danesh Mohiuddin

Owlkids Books acknowledges the financial support of the Canada Council for the Arts, the Ontario Arts Council, the Government of Canada through the Canada Book Fund (CBF) and the Government of Ontario through the Ontario Creates Book Initiative for our publishing activities.

Owlkids Books gratefully acknowledges that our office in Toronto is located on the traditional territory of many nations, including the Mississaugas of the Credit, the Chippewa, the Wendat, the Anishinaabeg, and the Haudenosaunee Peoples.

Published in Canada by
Owlkids Books Inc.
1 Eglinton Avenue East
Toronto, ON M4P 3A1

Published in the United States by
Owlkids Books Inc.
1700 Fourth Street
Berkeley, CA 94710

Library of Congress Control Number: 2022939171

Library and Archives Canada Cataloguing in Publication

Title: Princess Pru and the ogre on the hill / by Maureen Fergus ; illustrated by Danesh Mohiuddin.
Names: Fergus, Maureen, author. | Mohiuddin, Danesh, illustrator.
Description: Series statement: Oggy and Pru ; 1
Identifiers: Canadiana 20220251495 | ISBN 9781771475006 (hardcover)
Classification: LCC PS8611.E735 P75 2023 | DDC jC813/.6—dc23

Edited by Jennifer Stokes and Katherine Dearlove
Designed by Danielle Arbour

ONTARIO ARTS COUNCIL
CONSEIL DES ARTS DE L'ONTARIO
an Ontario government agency
un organisme du gouvernement de l'Ontario

Canada Council
for the Arts

Conseil des Arts
du Canada

Canada

Manufactured in Shenzhen, Guangdong, China, in October 2022 by WKT Co. Ltd.
Job # 22CB0154

MIX
Paper | Supporting
responsible forestry
FSC® C010256

A   B   C   D   E   F   G

Publisher of Chirp, Chickadee and OWL
www.owlkidsbooks.com

Owlkids Books is a division of

Princess Pru
and the Ogre
on the Hill

by Maureen Fergus

Illustrated by Danesh Mohiuddin

Owlkids Books

Princess Pru's life was practically perfect. She had two loving dads, an ostrich named Orville, and three royal tarantulas.

The only thing that kept Princess Pru's life from being *perfectly* perfect was the ogre who'd recently moved into the house on the hill.

He was hulking and hairy,
fearsome and scary.
His toenails were crusty.
His gray ears dripped goop.
And his breath stank like socks
dunked in rotten-egg soup.

Princess Pru didn't care that the ogre had crusty toenails and goopy ears. What she *did* care about was that he ruined . . .

her royal rock band rehearsals,

her weekly tickle tag games,

and even the royal
hide-and-seek tournament!

The day the ogre "attacked" the castle, Princess Pru began
to wonder if perhaps he was just lonely.

So she asked her dads if she could throw him a "Welcome to the Kingdom" party.

"Absolutely not!" cried King Karl. "Everyone knows that ogres hate seeing people have fun."

"Maybe everyone is wrong," said Princess Pru.

"Maybe," said King Knish. "But we're not taking any chances."

At first, Princess Pru assumed that her dads were being their usual overprotective selves. However, the palace soon began receiving alarming reports regarding the ogre's behavior.

On Monday, he went to the bakery and ordered ten dozen chocolate cupcakes with sprinkles on top.

On Tuesday, he went to the grocery store and filled his cart with potato chips, ice cream, and soda.

On Wednesday, he went to the craft store and stocked up on construction paper, glitter glue, streamers, and sparklers.

On Thursday, he went to the balloon store and bought three hundred balloons.

On Friday, he spent the day at home vacuuming, dusting, and decorating.

The people of the kingdom were terrified.

"What could the ogre possibly be up to?" they cried. "What chilling act will he commit next?"

The chilling act the ogre committed next was to send everyone in the kingdom a handwritten note with an ominous message . . .

"Being turned into ogre stew would be
a big surprise!" fretted King Knish.

"Being forced to trim an ogre's toenails would also be a big surprise," moaned King Karl. "Oh, what is that horrible ogre up to?"

Princess Pru had a pretty good idea what the ogre was up to. And that is why, shortly before two o'clock on Saturday, she put on her fanciest outfit, whistled for her ostrich, Orville, and headed for the house on the hill.

Her dads and all the people of the kingdom ran after her.

"Don't do it!" shouted the people of the kingdom.

"It's a trick!" warned King Karl.

"It's a trap!" wailed King Knish.

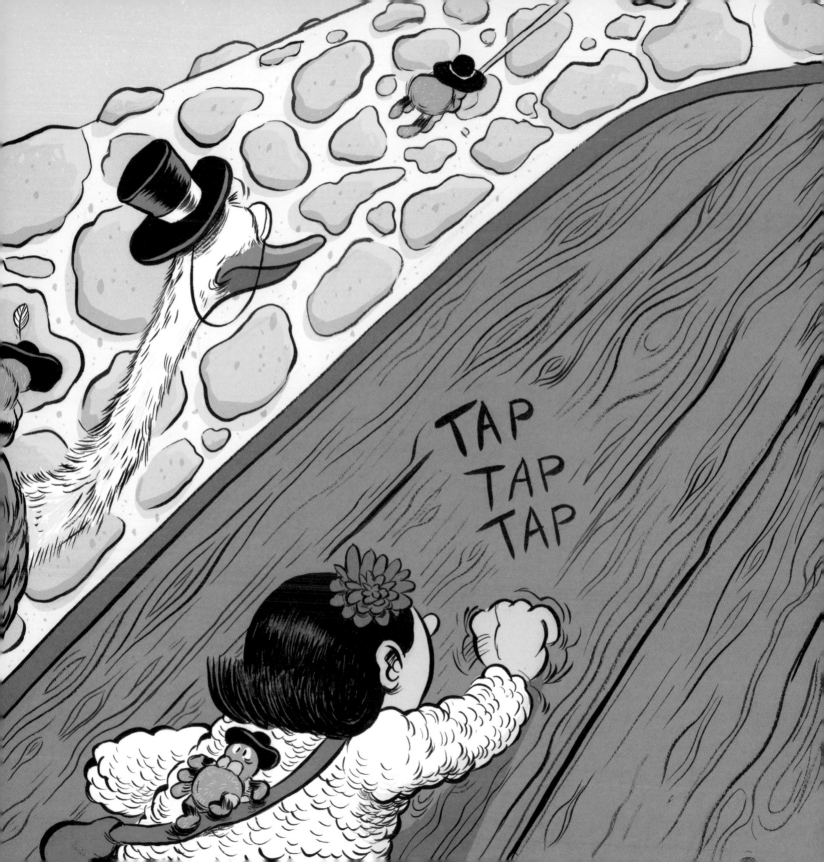

"Actually," said Princess Pru as Orville bounded up to the ogre's front porch, "I think it's a party."

Leaping off Orville, Princess Pru bravely stepped forward and knocked on the door.

"You came!" cried the ogre. "I wasn't sure you would, because everyone says that princesses don't like ogres. But that isn't true, is it?"

"No," said Princess Pru. "It isn't."

Princess Pru, her royal parents, Orville the ostrich, the people of the kingdom, and the ogre named Oggy spent the afternoon playing ogre games, making ogre crafts, and eating ogre-licious cupcakes.

It was the best party any of them had ever attended.

In the weeks that followed, Princess Pru discovered that Oggy was as good a friend as a royal princess could hope for.

He was faithful and funny,
*   helpful and sunny,*
A listener, a playmate,
*   a pal through and through,*
A kindhearted friend who
*   would always be true.*

And on top of all that . . .

. . . he was exactly what her royal rock band needed
to take their music to the next level!

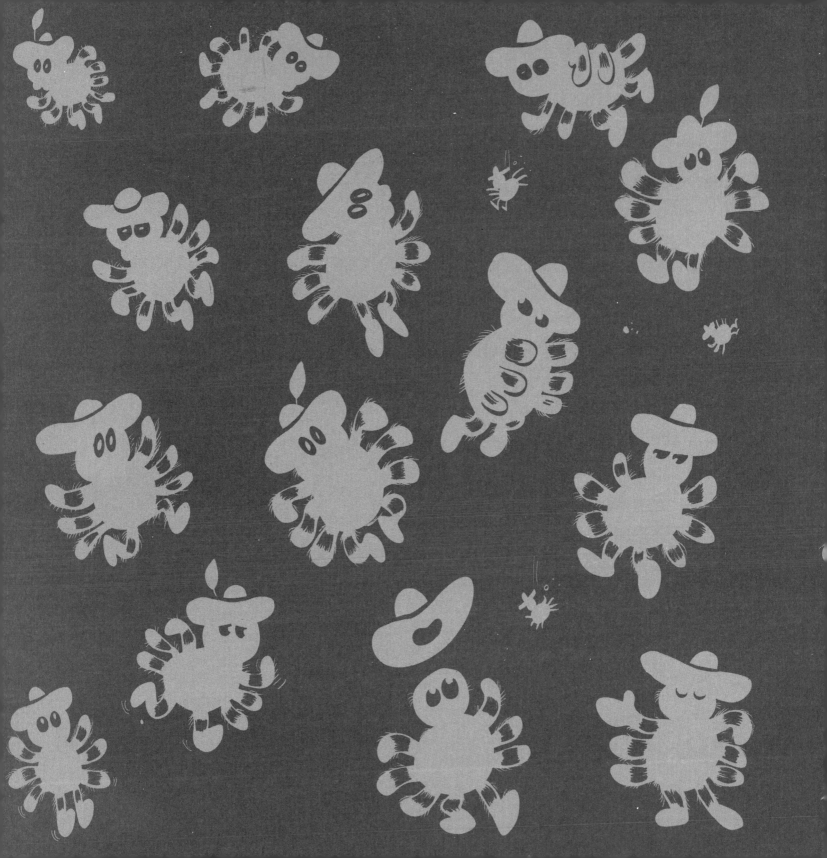